THIS BOOK BELONGS TO:

_____

_____

_____

For John

Thank you, mom, for all of the bedtime stories

Special thanks to
Dorothy and Lew Davis
Bruce and Sue Davis
Logan and Laura Bryant (and Little Squirt)
Paul and Jackie Hutchison
Ben Slad
Chicago Teach for America staff members:
George, Maire, Morgan, Jessica, Kiran,
Gregory, Heidi, Claire, Matea, Kelly,
Anne, Aditya, Laura, and Julianne

Thank you to all supporters of the Know It All Nori Kickstarter Project

Text copyright © 2015 by Elizabeth Hereford
Illustrations copyright © 2015 by Elizabeth Hereford
Published by Elizabeth Hereford

Printed in China

ISBN-10: 0692389040
ISBN-13: 978-0-692-38904-1

# Know It All Nori
# The Holiday Song

By Elizabeth Hereford

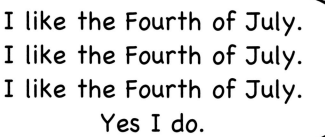

# The Holiday Song
to the tune "Alluette"
repeat for all verses

I like Christ mas  I like Christ mas

I like Christ mas  Yes I do

I like trick or treat ing  I like wear ing cos tumes

I like Christ mas  Yes I do